MATCH-MAKING IN MONTANA

PAMELA M. KELLEY

UNTITLED

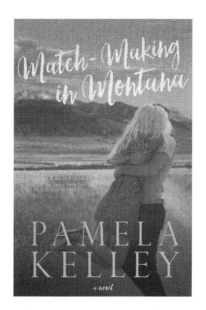

MATCH-MAKING IN MONTANA

If you'd like to receive my new release alerts, special promos, and more,
please sign up for my newsletter, http://eepurl.com/IZbOH

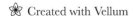 Created with Vellum

CHAPTER 1

"So, are you excited about tonight? What are you going to wear?" Isabella asked as she handed a freshly poured cup of coffee to Anna and then shut the conference door behind them. Almost every day, sometime between two and three, they always tried to catch up for a quick coffee break. They'd met years ago when both had started working at the real estate office in downtown Beauville soon after college. Anna was newly married then, and although she and Isabella had gone to the same high school, they were a year apart and didn't really know each other. They'd clicked instantly and had been best friends ever since. Isabella worked in sales and was one of their top agents, while Anna was the office manager and oversaw all the accounting and administrative work to keep the office running smoothly.

"I only have a few minutes. I have to run out to the bank still and then bring some documents to the registry of deeds," Anna said as she sat down.

Isabella leaned back in her chair and tapped her perfectly manicured nails against the table.

"I have to go in a minute, too, but stop avoiding the question. Talk to me about tonight."

Anna sighed. She wished she could be even half as excited as Isabella was about this date.

"Just be open-minded. Try to have fun," Isabella urged.

"I will, I promise." Doug did seem like a nice enough guy and they were meeting at her favorite restaurant, Delancey's.

"He was the best out of the first batch. I'm working on a few others for you."

Anna chuckled. "I still can't believe you put a profile up without telling me."

Isabella took a sip of coffee and then shot her a look. "Oh please. Like you would have done anything your-self? You'd still be spending your evenings with Ben & Jerry."

"You're right." Anna smiled. "They are good company, though."

Isabella had taken it upon herself to post a profile on the biggest dating website in Montana, Match-Making.-com. She'd posted as if she was Anna, and only shared Anna's pics with men that she deemed worthy. She even handled the email exchanges until it got to the point where the men wanted to meet her, and then she presented them to Anna. Doug was the first one who Anna agreed to meet with in person, because after looking over Doug's profile and the email exchanges, she couldn't find any good reason to say no. He seemed like a nice enough guy.

"Besides, it's just drinks and maybe an appetizer or two. No pressure," Isabella reminded her. Anna had insisted that dinner was too much for what was essentially a blind date. Drinks, and maybe if it was going well, an appetizer. That she could do.

"It will be fun," Anna tried to convince herself. She hadn't been on a date in well over a year. Getting divorced had been one of the hardest things she'd ever done. Difficult, but necessary once she'd discovered that her husband of more than fifteen years was cheating—with multiple women over a two-year period. He tried to convince her it was just a mid-life crisis, that it would never happen again, and for a very brief moment she considered taking him back. But, she couldn't do it. Ultimately, she knew she could never trust him again and her attraction to him was gone. But still, she mourned the death of the relationship that they'd had for so many years and a love she'd thought would last forever.

"Call me when you get home. I don't care how late it is."

"It won't be late. It's a school night. I don't like to leave the boys by themselves for too long," She said, though they were certainly old enough to be home alone for a few hours. She just never did because she never went anywhere.

"This will be good for you. Even if it's not a love connection, at least you're trying and getting out there again. It will get easier," Isabella assured her.

"I hope so." Anna glanced at the clock on the wall. "I'd better run. See you in a bit."

———

AFTER ANNA LEFT, ISABELLA WENT BACK TO HER DESK AND checked emails while waiting for her next client to arrive. One of the emails was from her husband Travis, who worked as a lawyer and had an office right up the street. He was checking to see what time she'd be finishing up, as his best friend, Christian, and his wife, Molly, wanted to have them over for dinner. Christian's brother, Dan, and his wife, Traci, would probably be coming, too. Isabella immediately replied that she'd make sure she finished up in time. It would be fun to see them all and she wasn't much of a cook, so she and Travis probably would have just ordered take-out anyway. This would be much more fun. Plus, Isabella was just over four months pregnant and while she wasn't showing yet, she was usually exhausted by the time she got home at night, so not having to worry about dinner was a good thing.

At a quarter to three, Isabella heard the front office door open and guessed it must be her new client. They had an appointment at three to see the only two rental listings that they currently had. When she'd spoken to him yesterday, she'd liked the sound of his voice and wondered if he might be a potential prospect for Anna, too. From some of his comments, she guessed that he was about their age and it sounded like he was going to be in the area for at least a year.

"Mr. Shelton?" she asked as she walked into the reception area.

"Yes, but please call me Zach." He shook Isabella's hand and she took a quick mental snapshot. The man standing before her was at least six two or six three, with a solid, athletic build, dark brown hair and deep brown eyes.

"As I mentioned on the phone, we're a bit low on rental inventory at the moment, but I do have two nice options to show you and both are immediately available. I can tell you more about them in the car."

Zach followed her outside and while Isabella drove to the first rental, she went over the details of both listings again with him.

"The first one I'm showing you is a modern, two-bedroom condo. It's a great location, just a few minutes from downtown, so very convenient. What kind of business did you say you were in?" Isabella wondered what had brought him to Beauville.

"I don't think I did say. I'm here for a consulting project of sorts." He didn't explain further, so Isabella went ahead and told him about the second rental.

"It's probably more than you need, but it's a lovely, large house in a good area, close to schools and just a little further out of town. It has a very large lot." It was an absolutely gorgeous house and it also happened to be located right next door to Anna's place. It had just come on the market a few days ago and Isabella knew it would go quickly. As much as she loved the thought of him living next to Anna, she highly doubted he would choose the house over the condo. As a single business man, the condo was much more practical.

Zach was quiet as they walked through the condo. There was nothing terribly exciting about it. The walls were beige, the floors were hardwood, the rooms were large so that was good, and it had two full bathrooms. It was really perfect for what he needed.

"That is certainly a good option," Zach said as they got back into the car and headed to look at the house. He didn't say much more as his attention was focused on the steady stream of text messages he was receiving and sending. His phone buzzed several times but he didn't answer it, and seemingly each call was followed by a text. He seemed to be one of those serious, type A business guys. So, Isabella's hopes for a match with Anna faded a bit. She really didn't see Anna with a cold, corporate businessman. She was much too warm and nice.

Anna really did live in a lovely neighborhood. It was set up high and had gorgeous views of the mountains and valley below. When Isabella pulled into the rental's driveway, the house looked warm and welcoming. It was somewhat contemporary in style with large windows to take in the views, an impressive, granite chef's kitchen, three oversized bedrooms upstairs and a guest bedroom or office on the main level. There was also a mahogany wood deck off the back. They walked outside, and Zach ran his hand along the meticulously polished wood.

"This is excellent quality. It's very soft to the touch." He sounded impressed.

Isabella reached out, lightly touched the wood railing

and agreed. It had almost a silky patina to it. There would be no splinters on that deck. They walked back inside to where Isabella had set her purse and folder on the kitchen island. "So what did do you think?"

"I'll take it."

"What? This one? You're sure?" Isabella had been certain it would have been the condo.

"I'm sure. This place is great. That condo was pretty sterile." He grinned then, and Isabella caught a glimpse of his personality. It was nice to know he had one. Maybe there was hope here yet. She was curious to discover what Anna would think of her new neighbor.

"Great. I have the lease forms with me. All I need from you is a check."

———

ANNA WAS BACK FROM HER ERRANDS AND IN HER OFFICE when Isabella knocked on her door, then walked in holding what looked like a rental lease.

"I have some interesting news for you," she began.

"Oh?" Anna looked up from the spreadsheet she was working on.

"I rented the house next to you to a seriously hot guy. He's a corporate type, but he might have potential."

"Really?" The house next door had been vacant for over a year while the owners traveled. It would be nice to see some life there again.

"You could be just a little bit more excited." Isabella seemed disappointed at her lack of enthusiasm.

Anna chuckled. "Sorry. But I do have a date tonight. That's a big step for me."

"I know," Isabella sighed. "I just want you to have what I have with Travis. We need to find you a good guy." She handed Anna the lease to be processed and turned to head back to her desk.

Anna glanced down at the lease and the name of her new neighbor. She felt suddenly light-headed and her stomach flipped. Could there be more than one?

"What does this Zachary Shelton look like?" she asked.

Isabella turned around and smiled. "Easy on the eyes, tall, brown-hair, dark eyes. No ring, either."

"Did he say where he's from?"

"Not really. Just that his main office is in Billings and he'll be working here for most of the next year. Some kind of consulting project."

"Did he look at all familiar to you?" The Zachary Anna was thinking of had been two years ahead of them in school. His family moved out of state after he graduated, so Isabella might not have known him.

"No, he didn't. Why, do you think you might know him?"

"Maybe. Though it could be a different person, I suppose. If it's the one I'm thinking of, I haven't seen him in almost twenty years. We were high school sweethearts and talked about getting engaged once we graduated from college. But, when he moved and started college, I never heard from him again. He was supposed to write as soon as he got settled, but he never did."

"Do you really think it could be that Zachary?" Anna had briefly mentioned this story when they first met, many years ago. But she was already engaged to her now ex-husband then and it never came up again.

"I really don't know. I can't imagine why he would come back here now, after all these years."

CHAPTER 2

Zach wandered into the lobby of the Rose Cottage a few minutes past five. When he'd checked in earlier that afternoon, Molly, the manager of the bed and breakfast, had told him to be sure to come by for happy hour in the main lobby between four and six. There were already a few people gathered by a long table that held several bottles of wine, a platter of cheese and crackers and a bowl of nuts. Zach was more of a beer drinker but did enjoy a glass of red wine every now and again. When he reached the table, two women in their sixties were standing by the wine.

"Hello, young man. What can we pour you? I'm Betty, Molly's aunt, and this is Susan, her mother."

"Nice to meet you both. I'd love a glass of red, please."

Susan poured a glass of wine and Betty handed it to him.

"So, are you here on business or pleasure?" Betty asked.

"Business, mostly. But I'm going to be in Beauville for a while. I'm just here for a few days, until I can move into my rental." He smiled and took a sip of wine. It woke up his appetite and his stomach rumbled. He'd just grabbed an apple on the run at lunchtime and was starving now.

"Can you ladies recommend a good place around here for dinner?"

Both women said, "Delancey's," at the same time, and then laughed. "There's just a few choices here in town and Delancey's is definitely the best one. Especially if you're good and hungry," Betty said.

He chatted with the women while he finished his wine and then headed off to Delancey's. The restaurant was busy, but there were a few seats open at the bar, so he settled into one of them and ordered a beer.

"What do you recommend?" he asked when the bartender handed him a menu.

"Have you been here before?" The bartender looked as though he was trying to place him.

"No, never." Delancey's hadn't been around when Zach lived there.

"Okay, then. You have to get the steak. It's what we're famous for."

"Sounds good to me. Make it medium-rare, please."

The bartender went off to punch in his order and Zach glanced around the bar. Not a single face was familiar, although it had been nearly twenty years since he'd been in Beauville. Everything looked different to him.

The town had grown a lot over the years. He was betting it would continue to grow. He watched the hostess seat an attractive couple at a booth in his direct line of vision. Over the next fifteen or so minutes, as he slowly sipped his beer, he couldn't help but notice the couple. The woman was the type he always seemed to be drawn to—curvy and very pretty with long, fine blonde hair and a friendly smile. The man looked a bit nervous. He was in a suit and Zach guessed he did something boring, like accounting. He just had a dry look about him. It also looked like it might be a first date, with lots of awkward pauses.

Zach was feeling quite content about being able to relax by himself and not have to worry about making idle chit-chat. But then he looked their way again and was surprised to see the woman was outright staring at him, almost as if she knew him. But that couldn't be, because there was no way he would forget this woman. It was almost a bit unsettling, the way she seemed to look right through him. But, then realizing he'd caught her staring, she quickly looked away and asked her date a question.

Zach's meal arrived then, and he dug in. It was delicious. He finished quickly, declined a second beer, and stood to leave. He glanced at the couple in the booth as he walked toward the door and once again, the woman was watching him—with an odd expression upon her face.

"Tom and Dylan, I have a hot rotisserie chicken and mashed potatoes that I just picked up at the market and I can make you either broccoli or green beans. What do you want?"

Tom, Anna's older son at nearly fifteen, and Dylan, who was twelve, were sprawled out on sofas in the family room. Though they both had textbooks open, Anna knew they were likely playing games on their smart phones.

"Mom, I hate chicken," Tom complained.

"Me, too," Dylan echoed, and then added, "Can we have mac and cheese instead?"

"Yeah, that would be cool," Tom agreed.

Anna hesitated. "Have you finished your homework? Both of you?"

"I finished mine." Dylan said and Anna believed him. Dylan was the organized one. He did his homework as soon as he got home and got it out of the way. Unlike his brother, who put it off until the last possible second.

"I'm almost done," Tom said.

"You're sure? If you get it done in the next half hour, I'll make you mac and cheese. Otherwise, you're stuck with the chicken."

Anna went upstairs to get dressed, and stood staring in her closet for a good ten minutes. She hated this part of dating, worrying about what to wear and what to say. It was all so uncomfortable, sometimes. A dress might seem like she was trying too hard, but jeans could be too casual. She finally settled on a favorite soft, blue sweater and gray dress pants.

After running a brush through her hair and adding a

sweep of blush to add some color to her face, she went back down to the kitchen and checked in with the boys. Tom swore that his homework was done, so she agreed to make the mac and cheese for them, and put the chicken away in the refrigerator. Twenty minutes later, she was out the door and heading to Delancey's where she'd told Doug she would meet him just inside the front door.

She spotted Doug immediately when she walked in. He looked just like his picture, except for seeming a little nervous.

"Anna?" he asked tentatively as soon as he saw her.

"Doug?"

"So nice to meet you." He leaned in and gave her an awkward hug.

"Shall we go in?" he asked, and she nodded. He opened the inside door and they walked toward the reception desk where he gave his name, and they were seated in a booth near the bar. Anna settled onto her seat and shrugged her coat off. The waitress came by a few minutes later, handed them menus and took their drink order.

"Do you like nachos?" Doug asked.

"I love them."

"Great, we'll order those, then. Do you see anything else we should get?"

"I think that will be plenty, unless you want something

else?" Anna wasn't very hungry, and nachos were the perfect thing to pick on.

When the waitress returned with their drinks, Doug put their order in and when she walked away, Anna glanced toward the bar and almost dropped the drink she was about to take a sip of. Zachary Shelton was sitting at the bar and looking her way. She felt his eyes connect with hers and she expected some kind of a reaction, but there was nothing. No recognition whatsoever. Quickly, she glanced away and forced her attention back to Doug and what he was saying.

"So, how has your experience been with Match-Making.com so far? Have you gone on many dates?"

Anna's heart was racing and she was completely discombobulated. Zachary looked completely the same, yet different. Older, and better. Any traces of a baby face were gone, replaced by a strong jaw and a sense of maturity. She wondered if she looked the same to him. She knew she'd put on a few pounds over the years, but she liked her curves and her hair was still long and blonde. He should have recognized her. She realized she was peeved that he hadn't. She wanted to march over to him and see if he recognized her up close, but that, of course wasn't possible.

"No, you're the first, actually," she admitted to Doug and smiled, trying to get mind her off the man at the bar.

"Really? I guess I should be honored, then." He took a sip of his beer and looked like he was trying to think of something else to say.

"What about you? What has your experience been

like so far?" Anna really didn't care to know about his history on the dating site. She felt like it was really none of her business, but it seemed to be one of the first questions men always asked in the email exchanges and it was something to talk about.

"I've gone on a few dates over the past couple of months. Nothing has worked out yet, though. Some people don't seem to use recent pictures." He frowned, obviously remembering a particularly unsuccessful date. "You did, though. You look even prettier than your picture."

"Thank you." The waitress returned a few minutes later with their nachos and set the huge platter down between them.

While they ate, Anna learned that Doug was once engaged but his girlfriend of five years had broken off the engagement a few weeks before the wedding, and then a month later, moved in with his best friend.

"It took a while to get over that one. Obviously, he's not my best friend anymore."

Anna sympathized and told him about her ex-husband.

"He was cheating on me with multiple women and I had no idea. I thought things were fine."

"I bet that took some time to get over, too," Doug said as he lifted up a chip that was smothered with melted cheese, chili and sour cream.

"It did. If it wasn't for my best friend, Isabella, I probably wouldn't be here now. She pushed me to do this, to get back 'out there', as she put it."

Their conversation grew more comfortable as they finished the nachos. Doug was a nice guy, and Anna learned that he really loved his job as an accountant. He'd been with the same company in Beauville for ten years and he owned a small condo in town. He grew up in Bozeman and moved to town after graduating from college and accepting a job offer here.

As pleasant as he was, though, Anna realized sadly that there wasn't any kind of a spark there for her. Doug fell firmly into the friend category. She told herself she was being too picky and that she should really try harder to feel something, and then she saw Zach coming her way as he headed toward the door. He glanced at her and once again, their eyes met. But still, there was no hint of recognition from him as he just as quickly glanced away and a moment later was gone. Even after all these years, though, Anna's heart was racing. There was no doubt that there was definitely some kind of a spark there, even if it was just on her side. Just knowing she could have that kind of a reaction to someone confirmed that it wouldn't be fair to go out with Doug again. Assuming, of course, he even asked.

When the bill came, Anna offered to put money in but he wouldn't hear of it.

They walked out together and when they reached Anna's car, Doug gave her a quick hug.

"It was really nice to meet you. I'd love to go out again sometime. Drop me a note if you are up for it."

"It was really nice to meet you, too. Thanks for the nachos."

Anna climbed in her car and started the engine. If she hadn't seen Zach at the bar would she have felt differently about Doug, she wondered? Sadly, she realized probably not. The spark was either there nor not, and it just wasn't there for her with Doug.

CHAPTER 3

Isabella answered the phone on the first ring. "So, how did it go? Did you like him? I've been wondering all night."

"I saw Zach." Anna had waited to call Isabella until she got home, checked on the boys, then got into her pajamas and climbed into bed.

"What? Did you talk to him? What about Doug?"

"Zach was sitting at the bar. He looked right at me and it was like he'd never seen me before. It was really weird." Anna paused, and then added, "I don't look that different, do I?"

"He didn't recognize you? That is strange. No, I think you look almost the same—better, even."

"You're biased." Anna laughed. "And I love you for it."

"What about Doug? Could there be a possible love connection there?"

Anna sighed. "No, and it's too bad. He's a really nice guy."

"No sparks?"

"Not even a hint."

"Zach looked good, though, didn't he?" Isabella asked.

"He did. I have to say it really kind of freaked me out that he looked right at me, twice, and there was no hint of recognition. I know I have put on some weight." Anna was trying to make sense of it.

"You're not the least bit overweight. You have a great figure."

"Maybe he just forgot about me. I obviously wasn't as important to him as he was to me."

"Maybe he needs glasses. Or it was dark in the restaurant. It might be something simple like that," Isabella pointed out.

"I suppose."

"Don't worry about it. He's going to be living right next door. Maybe when you bump into him in the daylight, he'll remember you."

"Maybe." Anna doubted it somehow. Maybe he didn't want to remember her. After all, he did move away and then fell off the face of the earth. Maybe his idea of 'together forever' had changed.

"So, Doug is out. When you come in tomorrow morning, I have someone new to show you. Brad is interested in meeting for coffee next Thursday. Does that work for you?"

"What? Can we talk about this tomorrow?" Sometimes Isabella was hard to keep up with.

"Sure thing. Get a good night's sleep. And don't worry about Zach."

"I'M COMING IN FOR THE DAY NEXT WEDNESDAY. YOU CAN tell Mr. Davenport I'll see him then." Zach kept an eye on the street signs as he spoke. He was about a mile away from where he was going.

"I'll make it happen. Do you want it to be a lunch meeting?" Ashley, Zach's executive assistant, had been with him for three years now and she was a godsend.

"No. I don't want to spend that much time with him. I thought you and I could have lunch, actually, and you can bring me up to speed on anything I'm missing."

"Absolutely. The Carlyle?"

Zach chuckled to himself. Ashley would suggest the best restaurant in the city.

"Sure, why not. Thanks, Ash." He hung up and turned off the main road onto a dirt driveway. The road seemed to go on forever. It was at least ten minutes before he reached his destination. He hadn't been here in a very long time. Zach parked the car, left his phone on the seat and walked toward the small house.

To say he was surprised to get the call about this property was an understatement. His mother and uncle had had a major falling out many years ago, long before he and his mother moved out of state. When she died, his uncle came to the funeral but Zach hadn't seen him in well over ten years at that point, and he was like a stranger. After the service, they both mumbled something about keeping in touch, but Zach never heard from him again. The call came a few months ago that he had passed on and since he had no children of his own, he'd left everything to Zach.

The attorney who called him also explained that the small house that his uncle had lived in was in need of major repairs. The house was over fifty years old and the plumbing had never been replaced. If Zach was planning to sell, the attorney advised him, that would need to be taken care of and brought up to code first. The attorney had assumed that Zach would probably put the property on the market and was surprised to hear that he planned to keep it, at least for the time being.

The most surprising thing about the attorney's first call had been that Zach's initial and immediate reaction was one of pure joy, followed by a strong urge to discover where that came from. He vaguely knew that he'd been happy in Beauville and this seemed like a sign of sorts to go and spend some time there. Billings was only a few hours away, yet in the five years he'd been living there, he hadn't been back to Beauville once. There really hadn't been a reason to go back. It had been so long since he'd lived there that he'd lost touch with everyone from those days, especially after the accident.

The property included a hundred acres, which was tiny compared to some of the cattle ranches in the area, but still a large amount of land. It was mostly buildable acreage, and Zach's practical side knew it made sense to sell and pocket the money. But Zach wasn't inclined to sell. He didn't really need the money. His company was five years old, and four years ago, he'd bought out his college roommate and business partner who had tired of it by then. It wasn't an easy business, but Zach was good at it and it paid very well. He could afford to keep this land if he wanted to—and he was pretty sure that he wanted to.

WHEN ANNA GOT HOME FROM WORK THE NEXT DAY, SHE noticed a gray Range Rover in the driveway next door. The back of the car was open and there were several large, cardboard boxes on the ground. It looked like Zach was moving in. Anna waited for a moment, curious to see if he'd be right back out, but after sitting there for a few minutes with no sign of him, she shut off the engine and went inside.

Isabella had shown her Brad's information as soon as she'd walked in the door that morning. Isabella had completely moved on from Doug and on to the next candidate, which was Brad. He looked like a good possibility—on paper anyway. His picture was attractive. He was a little taller than average height, maybe five ten or so, and had sandy, blond hair and blue eyes. He worked in IT, as a network engineer fixing computer issues for local Beauville customers. Anna agreed to meet him Thursday before work, for coffee at The Morning Muffin, the best coffee shop in Beauville. She actually liked the idea of meeting for coffee instead of after-work drinks. It seemed a little more casual.

Anna put an already cooked tray of lasagna in the oven to heat up, then realized she'd forgotten to bring in the mail. She liked to go through the mail every day and get any bills that needed to be paid taken care of as soon as possible. Maybe it came from handling all the office bills, but she had a fear of missing something and being late. Keeping her credit as strong as possible was very important to her. Her ex-husband hadn't been as concerned about it, and early in their marriage his behavior had badly damaged their credit. Anna wasn't going to let that happen again. She slipped on her shoes and coat and ran outside to grab the mail from the box at the end of the driveway.

Zach was by his car. She saw him immediately as she stepped outside. His garage door was open and he was moving the boxes inside. She walked to her mailbox, got the mail and slowly walked back, wondering what to do. Should she go talk to him? It would certainly be strange to introduce herself to him, as if they were strangers. Maybe Isabella was right and he'd recognize her now, although it wasn't exactly full daylight anymore. The sun was fading fast and it would soon be dark. He saw her as she drew near and smiled.

"Hi, there. Looks like we are going to be neighbors." When Anna reached him, he put out his hand and said, "I'm Zachary Shelton."

"Anna Stevens," she said as she shook his hand. It felt totally surreal to be introducing herself to Zach.

"It's nice to meet you, Anna." Zach smiled again and his eyes lit up, a familiar look that used to melt Anna's heart. Now, it just confused her. He really didn't remember her. How could that be?

"What brings you to Beauville?" she asked, curious why he was here now, after all these years.

"I grew up here, and moved away right after graduating from high school. I haven't been back since, but my uncle recently passed away and I inherited his place here. I'm not totally sure what I'm going to do with it, but while I'm deciding, I'm going to renovate his old house and work remotely for a while."

"I'm sorry to hear about your uncle. Were you close?" She didn't recall him ever saying much about an uncle.

"No, I don't think so. He and my mother hadn't talked in years."

"You don't remember if you were close to him?" That seemed like an odd statement.

Zach hesitated, as if trying to decide how much to say.

"I was actually in a car accident just a few weeks after I moved away from here. It was a bad one, and I was in the hospital for a very long time. My mother died on impact. I had a pretty serious head injury and my memory was affected. Pretty much wiped clean, actually."

"You lost your memory? You don't remember anything about living here in Beauville?" Anna couldn't believe it. It sounded too crazy.

"I don't remember much at all, just little random bits and pieces, an overall sense that I liked it here, a lot."

"Why haven't you been back until now?" Surely, he must have been curious?

"If not for this inheritance, I probably wouldn't have come back. I didn't want to run into people and have them recognize me and me not have any idea who they were. I'm just hoping that enough time has passed now that even if they did know me back then, they won't recognize me now. Or maybe they'll just think I look familiar but not put two and two together."

"Have you run into anyone yet who knows you? Or that looks even a little familiar?"

"No. I haven't been here long, though. I'm sure I will, at some point."

"You have now," Anna said tentatively. She didn't want to lie to him and pretend she didn't know him, but she also wasn't sure how much she wanted to share about how well they had known each other.

"Really? You knew me back then?" Zach looked surprised and a bit wary.

Anna smiled. "Yes, we were in the same grade."

"How well did we know each other?" Anna saw the turmoil in Zach's eyes, the fear of the unknown and she decided to put him at ease.

"We were friends, actually, and had a few classes together. You were much better at math than I was." That was true. Zach had excelled in math and he used to help her with her calculus homework.

"I can see that. Math always came easily to me." He

was quiet for a moment and then asked, "What was I like then?"

Anna had to think about how much to share at this point. "You were very focused, got excellent grades, ran track, did well on the debate team and had a lot of friends. I was one of them."

"That's good to hear. And nice to know I have a former friend for a neighbor."

Anna shivered then, finally noticing the cold outside, and Zach noticed, too. "I'm sorry, I won't keep you. I look forward to catching up and getting reacquainted."

"Me, too." Anna hugged her coat tightly around her and turned to go inside. "Goodnight, Zach."

CHAPTER 4

The cute woman from the restaurant was his next-door neighbor and she knew him from high school. Zach watched Anna walk back into her house and tried to wrap his head around what he'd just learned. No wonder she'd been looking at him at Delancey's. Probably thought he was a rude bastard for not recognizing her. It was the strangest thing, though. When he was talking to Anna and she told him they knew each other, he expected to feel something, some kind of ah-ha moment in his brain, linking his buried memories to this new information. But, there was nothing. Well, not completely nothing. The attraction Zach had felt in the restaurant was even stronger now that he'd actually talked to Anna.

Zach wasn't looking to start any kind of a relationship, though, as he wasn't sure how long he was going to stay in Beauville. Just from his brief interaction with her, he also knew that Anna wasn't someone he could have a casual fling with, especially if she already considered him a friend. Plus, she had children. He'd noticed the two boys earlier when they got off the bus. He wondered if there was a Mr. Stevens. Somehow he didn't think so, as he'd also noticed that she wasn't wearing a ring. No, he would fight his attraction to his very tempting neighbor. He liked the idea of having a friend in Beauville.

ANNA CHECKED ON THE LASAGNA WHEN SHE WENT BACK inside. It still had a while to go, probably a good twenty minutes, anyway. So, she decided to do something she rarely did during the week and not all that often on the weekends, either. She opened a bottle of good, red merlot and poured herself a glass. The boys had the TV going while they did their homework, so she decided to slip into the sunroom and relax for a few minutes. The minute she sat down, she called Isabella and filled her in.

Isabella, who was seldom at a loss for words, was speechless for a long moment, before finally saying, "He has amnesia? Still? Is it normal for it to last that long?"

Anna had wondered the same thing. "Nothing about this is normal."

"And there was no glimmer of recognition, even when you told him who you were?"

"No. But I didn't tell him everything. I only said we were friends."

"So, he has no idea?"

"No. I didn't see the point. If he doesn't remember

me, why make him feel bad by telling him how great it was and how close we were."

"I suppose." Isabella didn't sound convinced. "But, what if telling him helps him to remember?"

"I thought about that, but then thought it might be more awkward to tell him and then he still remembers nothing. Especially with him living next door."

"That makes sense. He could probably use a friend here," Isabella agreed.

"Honestly, that's more my speed these days, anyway. I still just don't feel that excited about dating," she admitted.

"You will. You just need to get used to it again and have fun. Go on a bunch of dates and take your time getting to know people," Isabella advised.

"Hmmm, I don't know about dating a lot of people at once. I don't know if I could do that. I do like the idea of going slow, though."

"Well, you don't have to date more than a few at once, but it really does help to have several people you are going on dates with."

"Why?" It sounded stressful to Anna.

"That's what all the dating experts advise, that you should have a 'pair and a spare'. Two guys you like and a back-up guy, so you always have someone to go out with and you never get too attached to any of them. Not until you figure out which one you really like, and by then, they're crazy about you, too. Because you're dating several guys, you won't always be available and that drives guys crazy. Makes them want to see you more."

Anna chuckled. "You make it sound like a sure-thing, scientific formula for successful dating."

"Well, it makes sense to me. Why not try it? There's another cute guy who seems interested, Cody. He's a cowboy. Works on the biggest ranch in the area."

"I've never dated a cowboy."

"First time for everything," Isabella said with a laugh.

An image of Zach in a cowboy hat came to Anna's mind instantly. When they were in high school, that had been his dream—to get his degree in agricultural science and then work on a ranch, and eventually run or own one himself.

"What is Zach doing here? He didn't really say the other day." Isabella asked and Anna smiled to herself. They did that all the time, said something that matched what the other one was about to say or had been thinking.

"I'm not sure. We didn't talk about it. He just said he'd inherited his uncle's property, a bunch of land and a small house that needs a lot of work. He's going to renovate it, but after that, I'm not sure what his plans are."

Anna caught a whiff of lasagna then, which meant it was probably ready to come out of the oven. She told Isabella she'd see her in the morning and then went out to the kitchen to give the kids dinner. As they all ate, Anna's thoughts kept returning to Zach and his mysterious amnesia. Since it had been so many years now, she wondered if it was even possible for him to get his memories back and if he would ever remember how things had really been between them and how important they were to each other. She took a sip of wine, felt tears well up and she fought them back. She hadn't even thought of Zach for several years now. One conversation with him and all the emotions came rushing back. Maybe him being her neighbor wasn't such a good idea, after all. It already seemed hard.

───────

THERE WAS A CHANCE OF SNOW THE FOLLOWING DAY, BUT it started earlier than expected, and by two p.m. there was close to six inches already accumulated and the winds were picking up. The original forecast was for just a few inches, but from what they'd just heard on the office radio, the storm had taken an unexpected turn and now they were facing the possibility of several feet of snow. Not that that was anything unusual in Montana. Anna had four-wheel drive on her Subaru SUV and snow tires, too, but she still got nervous driving in really bad weather. As Anna and Isabella stood by the main window watching the snow, Dee, the owner of the real estate office, walked over with a concerned expression.

"I don't know about you girls, but I've had enough snow for today. Let's shut it down and all head home. Drive safe and plan on working from home tomorrow, if you have power."

Anna was relieved. If she left now, she might be home about the same time as the boys who, no doubt, were excited about the very good possibility of a snow day tomorrow.

"Aren't you so glad you splurged for that generator?" Isabella said as she gathered up her purse and notebook and got ready to head home.

"Best investment we've made," Anna agreed as she buttoned her coat and prepared to face the cold outside. Her ex-husband had insisted on having a full-house generator installed so they would never lose power and the TV would always be on. Anna had argued at first, protesting the expense that seemed extravagant to her, but eventually she gave in and as much as she'd hate to admit it to him, she was very glad to have that generator. She had a strong suspicion it might come in handy later.

Anna drove slowly home, and when she pulled onto her street, she saw the school bus just ahead of her. She waited as the boys got off the bus, then followed them into the driveway.

"Mom, you're home, too. Cool! Do you think we'll have a snow day tomorrow?" Dylan was excited about the prospect and Anna smiled. She'd loved snow days as a kid, too.

"It wouldn't surprise me. The wind is picking up and this is supposed to go through the night."

As she walked into the house with the boys, she noticed that Zach's car wasn't in his driveway, but his lights were on. She guessed that the car was in the garage and Zach was in for the night. She wondered if he had a generator.

THE WIND HOWLED FOR THE NEXT TWO HOURS WHILE THE snow fell so furiously that all they could see out the window was a wall of swirling white. Anna had her laptop on the kitchen island so she could keep an eye on email while she cooked. She loved to cook and found the repetitive chopping, dicing and stirring relaxing, and the smells intoxicating. Even though she had a generator, she didn't want to leave anything to chance, just in case something went wrong and it didn't switch on when the power went down. She got a few logs out of the garage and started a fire in the woodstove that sat in the corner of the kitchen. It was solid cast-iron and, although it wasn't very big, it generated a lot of heat.

She also had a gas stove so she'd still be able to cook, even without power, so that eased her mind a bit. She decided to make a hearty beef stew since she had all the vegetables and some meat that was already thawed out. It was perfect beef stew weather. Just as she was about to put the large pot in the oven for several hours, the lights flickered, dimmed and then a minute later came back full force. The generator had done its job perfectly. Anna turned on a back burner and set the pot on the stove top. It could simmer there instead.

Three hours later, it was a little past six and the storm was still raging outside. The power hadn't come back on yet, so Anna knew it was likely to be out now overnight, possibly for several days before crews could get up into the hills and make the necessary repairs. She walked over to a side window and looked for lights next door at Zach's place. It didn't look like he had a generator—she saw nothing but darkness in that direction.

"Dylan, honey can you come here a minute?" Anna called to her younger son, who was by far the more energetic of the two.

"What's up, Mom?"

"Do you want to do me a favor? Can you walk next door and ask Mr. Shelton if he'd like to join us for dinner? Tell him we have plenty of room if he wants to sleep here tonight. His house might be really cold soon."

"Sure, be right back."

"Don't forget your hat and mittens!" she called after him.

Less than ten minutes later, he was back, by himself.

"Was he home, honey?"

"Yeah, he said to tell you he'll be over soon."

CHAPTER 5

Z ach glared at the wood stove in his kitchen, kicking himself for not picking up wood earlier in the day for it. When he'd moved in, he had noticed that there was a solid-looking, wood-burning stove in the family room, but the plastic bin in the garage that looked like it had held wood was empty, except for a few small twigs. The temperature inside the house had already dropped quite a bit and his cooking stove was electric. He was out of luck for dinner, unless he wanted cereal with no milk, because he'd also forgotten to get that earlier, along with the peanut butter he'd meant to pick up. He would have to make a list and bring that to the store once the roads cleared up. He was just about to head upstairs to put on a warmer sweater when there was a knock at the door. Who the hell would be out in this weather?

He opened the door to see one of the boys from next door, the younger one.

"My mom said to invite you over for dinner and to tell you we have a generator and plenty of room if you want to stay with us tonight." The words came out in a rush. A generator. That was smart of her.

"I'd love to come for dinner. Tell your mom I'll be over shortly."

ZACH GRABBED A BOTTLE OF WINE FROM A RACK ON HIS counter, put on his coat and hat and stepped outside. The snow was still coming down heavily and blowing every which way. He was at Anna's door a minute later and knocked loudly. It flew open and Dylan was standing there.

"He's here, Mom."

"Invite him in, honey," Anna called from the kitchen. Zach could just barely see her from the doorway. It looked like she was tossing a salad.

"Can you give this to your mom?" Zach handed the bottle of wine to Dylan and took his coat and hat off, then followed him into the kitchen.

"You didn't have to bring anything," Anna said as Dylan handed her the wine.

"It was the least I could do. And it was all I had. Your timing was perfect. My choices were cereal with no milk or cold soup out of a can. Thank you."

"Well, we're having soup, too. Beef stew. But, it will be nice and hot." Anna smiled.

"It smells amazing."

"Thanks. It's just about ready, so we can sit down and eat in a minute. Do you want to open the wine?" Anna handed him a corkscrew and Zach opened the bottle of merlot, pouring a glass for each of them.

"Boys, dinner's ready," Anna called. She filled bowls with the beef stew, set out a plate of sliced bread and butter and the salad. Then they all sat down to eat.

Zach was impressed by how delicious the stew was. Anna was an amazing cook and her house had such a warm, welcoming feel to it with the woodstove crackling in the corner and throwing off tons of heat.

"You're a really good cook," he said, and Anna smiled.

"Thank you. I've always loved it."

"Well, anytime you want to try out a new recipe, let me know. I'm happy to be your guinea pig."

"I'll keep that in mind," Anna said with a chuckle. "So, you mentioned your uncle's house, but aside from that, what exactly is it that you are going to be doing here in Beauville in the coming months?"

"I'll be running my company, just remotely. I'm really looking forward to remodeling my uncle's old house. I was just out there yesterday. The bones of it are good, it mostly needs updating and some repairs."

"So mostly you're here to check out his property?

"Partly. I'm also honestly feeling an itch to own a working ranch. I figured, I could get a taste of it with my uncle's land and if it goes well, then I can expand and purchase additional acreage. It's something I've always been really drawn to," he admitted.

Anna opened her mouth as if she was about to say something, then stopped. Zach wondered what she had been about to say.

"Penny for your thoughts," he said, and was surprised to see a blush creep over her cheeks.

"What? Oh, it's nothing," Anna said, then asked, "So, tell me about Billings. Have you lived there long?"

"About five years. Was in Austin, Texas, before that. Went to school down there and then stayed for a few years after graduating. A buddy and I opened this business in Billings and it's done well. He wanted out, though, after a year or so. It just wasn't his thing, so I bought him out. It's a small business but I love it."

"And you can do it from here? Is it hard to work remotely?" Anna seemed intrigued by the idea.

"Are you thinking you might want to try it?"

Anna thought about that for a minute. "No, not really. I do like to go visit with people for a few minutes and I think it would probably just be easier for me to be there, to put out any fires that start."

"It's really not that hard. You just need to have a laser focus on what needs to be done."

"Do you ever have to meet with people?"

"Not too often. My assistant will schedule meetings for me one day a week, so I can just head up there the night before and then spend the day at the office."

After they finished eating, Anna cleared their plates and then they moved into the family room.

"Did Dylan tell you we have a spare bedroom? You

are welcome to sleep here tonight and tomorrow, too, if we're still without power."

"Thank you. Smart thinking to have a generator. I have one in Billings, too."

"I wish I could take credit for it, but it was my ex-husband's idea. I actually thought it was too expensive. Never have I been so glad to be wrong."

"Do you want some more wine?" Zach asked. His glass was empty and he wanted a drop more.

"Normally, I would say no to a second glass, but this is really good. And I have a strong feeling I will have the day off from work tomorrow." She grinned at that, and Zach felt a spark again. He knew it was a bad idea to date his neighbor, but it was so tempting.

THE EVENING FELT A BIT SURREAL TO ANNA. ZACH HAD been good company over dinner and when he'd mentioned his dream to own a working ranch, she'd almost blurted out how they'd talked about that so often, how Zach would get his degree in agriculture and then work on a ranch until someday they could own one themselves and live together as husband and wife.

After dinner, they made themselves comfortable in the family room. The kids were off in their rooms, probably playing video games, and Anna and Zach sat on opposite ends of the main sofa.

"Did you get a chance to work on a ranch at all?" She wondered if he had still majored in agriculture.

"I did. Every summer, and then for a few years after graduating. I had a double major, though, in Business as well, and got my MBA. After that, I was recruited to a consulting company that focused on the ranching industry, looking at how ranchers can be more strategic in how they do things, to maximize profits and sustainability."

"Is that what your business does?"

"Yes. After a number of years, my partner and I opened the office in Billings."

"So now you're itching to put into practice what you're advising people?" she guessed.

Zach looked at her with a curious expression on his face.

"Yes. That's exactly it. I love what I do but I'd love to get more hands-on with it."

They chatted easily for the next few hours, and to Anna it was interesting to see how Zach had changed and in many ways, stayed very much the same. He'd never been so business-focused and intense about things. Yet, when he spoke about wanting to be hands-on with the ranch, she saw the old Zach shine through as his face lit up and he seemed more relaxed and happy. She wondered how he would like being back in Beauville and if being in old, familiar surroundings might bring his memories back. She also wondered if there was anyone waiting for him back in Billings. He hadn't mentioned having a girlfriend or anyone significant.

"Do you remember anything about your time living in Beauville?" she asked. Although she knew it wasn't his fault or hers, she still couldn't help feeling hurt that he didn't remember her at all.

"Very little. I do remember an overall sense of happiness. I know I liked living here and I know the ranching was part of it, but I'm not sure exactly how it fit in. There's bits and pieces, little flashes of memory or feelings that come and go, but nothing yet that I can grab hold of and build on. It can be frustrating," he admitted.

"What did your doctors say about it? Do they expect you might eventually remember?"

"They don't really know. They said the mind is a tricky thing. It holds on to information or releases it on its own timetable. Sometimes it's helped along by other people or places that were part of those memories. That's another reason I am planning to be here for a while. I'm hoping some of those memories might come back, the longer I am here."

"That makes sense." Anna considered telling Zach more about their relationship, but hesitated and then decided it was too soon. She didn't want to force his mind to go where it wasn't ready to go yet. Better to just get to know him again, slowly. A lot of time had passed and they were different people now. Telling him the full truth of what they had been to each other might be too much for him and could be awkward with them living next door to each other. It could get in the way of their simply being friends, which is what Anna wanted.

Around ten, Zach yawned and she immediately felt the urge to do the same.

"I think I'm about ready to head to bed. You're stay-ing, right?"

Zach hesitated.

"Don't be silly. Stay. Your house is going to be ice cold. The guest bedroom is right next to the kitchen and the bed is all made up for you."

"Okay, if you're sure it's no trouble."

"It's no trouble. See you in the morning."

———

ANNA WOKE TO THE WONDERFUL SOUND OF THE RADIO, which meant the power was back on. She got out of bed and looked out the window. The sun was shining. It had stopped snowing and there was a snowplow making its way down their road. One good thing about living in Montana is that they were never surprised by storms like this. Unless there was a major storm and widespread outages, they were usually pretty efficient. School was canceled, though. Anna heard it announced on the radio and when she checked her cellphone, there was a message from Dee saying they were going to keep the office closed today and everyone could work safely from home.

Anna started a pot of coffee brewing and was trying to decide between eggs and oatmeal when Zach walked into the kitchen. He was dressed and looked ready to head out the door.

"Good morning. Want some breakfast? Coffee is just about ready."

"I'll have a cup of coffee, thanks. Looks like we're

back up, so I'm off after that."

Anna poured coffee for both of them and decided on a bowl of oatmeal and a banana.

"You sure you don't want something to eat?"

"No, thanks. I'm good." Zach finished his coffee just as Anna's oatmeal was ready.

"Thanks again for dinner last night and for putting me up."

"Anytime." Anna topped her coffee off and sat down at the kitchen table, with her breakfast.

"Well, I'd like to return the favor. Have you and the boys over sometime soon for dinner."

"We'd like that."

Zach left then and Anna turned her attention to her oatmeal. It was nice to just relax and not have to rush off to work for a change. She had really enjoyed hanging out with Zach the night before. There was none of the awkwardness that she usually felt on first dates. Not that it was a date—she just wished she could have that level of ease with some of these guys that Isabella was setting her up with. Or at least have some of the sparks she still felt when she was around Zach. She wondered if the attraction was all one-sided. If he felt anything at all when he was around her. If on some level of his subconscious, he might remember. Or if not, if he might be attracted without even knowing their history? There wasn't any sign of that. He'd been nothing but friendly, which, given the situation, was probably for the best. Anna just wished the attraction she'd felt so many years ago wasn't still there. But evidently it was.

CHAPTER 6

The following Wednesday, Zach had several client meeting in Billings in the morning and then met his executive assistant, Ashley, at noon at The Carlyle for lunch. The Carlyle was a bit extravagant, but Zach didn't mind. Ashley deserved it. She really did an amazing job for him and all of his clients loved her. His business hadn't missed a beat since he moved out to Beauville, and that was largely because of Ashley. They caught up on all pending business, and were on dessert when she reminded him of his two o'clock appointment, the one he was least looking forward to.

"I'm really sorry. She has just been hounding me to get on your schedule and it might just be easier for you to see her and set her straight." Ashley looked furious on his behalf. "She is still telling people you're engaged and wearing that ring!"

Zach sighed. "That might sort of be my fault," he admitted, and then went on to explain. "When I called off the engagement and and told Bethanne I was moving to Beauville for a year—as you can imagine, she didn't take it very well."

"Well, she was planning the wedding of the year. She told me the reception was going to be here and she wanted everyone to know it."

"She never told me that, but it doesn't surprise me." He'd met Bethanne at a charity gala and he had been attracted to her right away. She was a very pretty girl, very polished, with pale, blonde hair that fell to her shoulders in a classic bob and there was never a hair out of place. She looked a little like Anna, he realized. The hair color was similar, anyway, but Bethanne was a size zero. He knew this because she told him, often, and was proud of it. He'd frequently thought she was too skinny, but he never told her that. Bethanne was impressed by things like that. She liked that he was a successful business owner and she made it clear that when she married, she expected to be a stay-at-home wife and mother. Zach didn't have a problem with that. He just wasn't sure that she was the one he wanted to stay home with forever.

He enjoyed dating her and they did have fun together, but every so often he'd get the feeling that something was missing. Especially when he found that when she wasn't around, he didn't miss her, and that didn't seem like a good thing. His biggest mistake was dating her as long as he did. They were together for four years, and when she started leaving pictures of rings around his apartment, he got the hint. Most of his friends were getting engaged and he and Bethanne had been together so long that it just seemed like the next step, what was expected. He was happy enough with her to do it, he told himself. But almost immediately after popping the question he regretted it, and the feeling grew over the next few months. Finally, when the call came about his uncle's land in Beauville, it seemed like a sign and an opportunity for a fresh start.

"So, when I told her I thought we should end things, she was upset. Although I think she was more upset about not having the wedding than by not marrying me." Ashley nodded at that and he knew she agreed.

"So, why is she still telling people you're engaged?"

"Well, when I told her I was going to be moving to Beauville shortly, she really didn't like it. I think she could see everything slipping away, and I did feel badly about that. So, when she asked me if instead of officially breaking the engagement, we could just take a 'pause' and then see how we felt in a few months, I didn't really have the heart to say no. She was really just asking me to give it some time—to think about it, and that seemed fair enough."

"So, do you feel any differently now that you've been away? Do you miss her?" Ashley looked worried and Zach smiled. He loved that she was so protective of him.

"No. If anything, it solidified my decision, and I will let her know that."

"Good luck."

ZACH WAS AT A COFFEE SHOP AROUND THE CORNER FROM his office at two o'clock sharp, waiting for Bethanne to arrive. Ashley had told him that Bethanne had pushed hard for their meeting to be at The Carlyle as well, which Ashley thought was absurd.

"She just wants everyone to see you together there, so she can keep telling them she's engaged. I told her it was out of the question because you were already meeting me there for lunch, so she backed down." Zach smiled as he recalled Ashley's indignation. He checked the time on his cellphone; it was ten past two and still no Bethanne. He expected that, though. She was never on time for anything. He'd gone ahead and ordered their coffees and checked email on his phone while he waited. Finally, at almost 2:20, she came breezing in, full of apologies.

"I'm so sorry. It took forever to get a cab over here. It would have been much easier if we'd met at the Carlyle. I could have walked there." He stood to greet her and she gave him an air kiss on the cheek. "You look great!" she said as she settled into the chair across from him. Zach slid a coffee over to her.

"I ordered one for you. Milk, no sugar, half decaf?"

She smiled. "So sweet of you, and thoughtful. Thank you. So, how have you been? Have you missed me?"

Zach smiled tightly. Did he miss her? She didn't make it easy for him. They hadn't spoken once since he'd left Billings.

"It's going well, thanks. Keeping very busy. How have you been?"

"Oh, you know me. Always busy, too. The junior

league has a big event coming up soon, so I'm on that committee. Different places have been calling me, too, about wedding arrangements. The best places book really far ahead, so if we are going to go forward, we should lock in a date soon—especially if we want the Carlyle." When he was speechless for a moment, she continued. "Or wherever we decide. It's the same with all the best places."

Zach shook his head. It was like she hadn't listened to him at all. Maybe she thought if she just kept moving forward and making arrangements that he'd fall into place, too. He couldn't really blame her. After all, that's how they'd come to be engaged in the first place.

"Bethanne, I'm really sorry, but I meant what I said when we last spoke. I don't feel any differently now and I'm not going to change my mind. I think we should both move on. I think you're great. I just don't think it's right with us." He paused then, and then looked at her intently. "Honestly, I think you feel the same, too, if you're really truthful with yourself. You're not madly in love with me."

He saw a shift in her eyes then, acceptance that she understood this was it and anger that she wasn't getting her way. He knew she'd never actually agree with what he'd just said, even though he was sure that she was more upset about having to cancel the wedding plans.

"Fine. The engagement is over. But, I'm keeping the ring!" She looked at him defiantly. "I deserve it."

"Keep the ring, Bethanne. I don't care about it."

"HE SLEPT OVER? WELL, THAT'S CERTAINLY PROMISING. Are you sure you still want to go out with Brad?" Isabella leaned forward in her chair, excited about this new development. Anna stood up and shut the conference room door so no one would overhear them. Then she sat back down and took a sip of coffee. It was almost nine a.m. and they were catching up quickly before the day got underway.

"No, it's not like that at all. I was just being neighborly. We're friends. It would be too weird otherwise."

"I don't know. You do have a history."

"Well, true, but that's what makes it even weirder frankly. I'm the only one who knows about it and even if I were to tell him, it's still not the same as him knowing it himself."

"I suppose. I have to admit I was sort of hoping you might re-kindle things, especially since I thought he seemed like a good catch for you even before I knew who he was."

"I am looking forward to meeting Brad for lunch today." They'd emailed about meeting for coffee, and then Brad had suggested lunch instead. Anna liked the idea because lunch was for a more limited time, too, so it should be less intimidating. Lunch options in Beauville were limited. Brad had left the choice of where to go up to her. For two seconds she considered Delancey's, but she rejected it as too fancy and possibly too slow if they wanted to get in and out in an hour. So, she suggested The Morning Muffin. It was more casual and they had great sandwiches and salads.

"I'll expect a full report later this afternoon," Isabella said.

"Of course. Just come grab me when you're ready for coffee. I'll be in my office.

ANNA STOPPED IN THE RESTROOM OF HER OFFICE BEFORE heading out. She smoothed hair and added a bit of lip gloss. Then she crossed the street and walked two blocks to The Morning Muffin. It was always busy there and today was no exception. The lunch rush was starting. Anna looked around the room and then recognized Brad at a corner table. She joined him and sat down. The Muffin had a takeout counter and also waitress service on the other side of the restaurant where they were sitting. Within minutes, Barbara, an older waitress who had worked there forever, came by to get their order. Brad ordered a turkey sandwich and Anna got her usual salad with grilled chicken.

"So, thanks for meeting me," Brad said as soon as Barbara walked away.

"This worked out well," Anna said. "My office is right around the corner."

"So you mentioned that you grew up here?" Brad asked.

"Yes, born and raised."

"And you stayed here. Did you ever think of moving away?" Anna liked that he asked thoughtful questions, not just the typical, "What do you do?"

"I did go away, to college. But then after graduating, I got married and we both found jobs here right away, so we stayed. What about you?"

"My family is in Bozeman, so I grew up nearby, too, and really never had any desire to live anywhere else. It's beautiful here. Plus I love the outdoors, hiking, kayaking, skiing. Do you ski?"

Anna laughed. "Yes, but poorly. I can get down the mountain, that's about it. My boys love it, though, especially snowboarding."

Barbara returned a few minutes later with their meals, and over lunch they discovered that they shared a few similar interests. Both of them loved going to the movies and playing cards, and although Brad had never been married, he did have several nieces and nephews that he was really close to and it was clear that he liked being around kids. Anna was very protective of her boys and dating someone who didn't like kids wasn't something she'd consider.

The lunch hour flew, and when the check came Anna reached for her wallet, and Brad immediately said, "I've got this."

"Thank you."

"It's my pleasure." He paused for a moment then, and said, "I really enjoyed this. I'd love to go out again, if you're up for it?"

"I'd like that," Anna said, and realized she meant it. She had enjoyed Brad's company and found him attractive, too. It wasn't the intense attraction she'd felt for Zach, but she really wasn't sure she'd ever find that level of attraction with anyone else. She would like to get to know Brad better and see if that attraction could grow.

———

"So, I saw something interesting while you were out," Isabella began when they caught up later that afternoon. Isabella had been out most of the day on showings, and as soon as she walked back in the office, she came straight into Anna's office.

"What's that?" Anna was endlessly entertained by Isabella, who seemed to find drama everywhere she went.

"Well, I was stopping off at the post office and on my way out, Zach was walking in, but he was distracted by something. He had stopped and was staring, so I looked where he was looking and guess what he was so interested in?"

"What?"

"You and your date walking out of The Morning Muffin."

"Really? You both saw me? How come you didn't say anything?"

"I wasn't going to interrupt your date! Just thought it was fascinating how interested Zach seemed to be."

"Maybe he was just bored. Not much going on in Beauville." So, why did this news give her a warm glow?

"Right. So, how was it? The date? Do you want to see this one again?"

"Actually, I do. Brad was really nice. We like a lot of the same things and he said he wants to go out again."

"Really?" Isabella looked surprised and pleased.

"You seem shocked," Anna teased her.

"Not that he'd want to go out again, just that you are finally interested, too. That's great! When are you going to see him again?"

"We talked about Friday night, possibly. He said he'll be in touch to confirm."

"Wonderful!"

CHAPTER 7

Zach couldn't stop thinking about Anna and wondering what she was up to. He'd never been so drawn to someone before and wasn't sure what to make of it. After he'd wrapped up work for the day, which was a little earlier than usual since it was a Friday, he went to the market and picked up some food for the weekend. He was going to see if Anna and the boys had plans that night and if they felt like coming over for dinner. He wasn't much of a cook, but he could grill a steak.

He saw Anna as he pulled into his driveway. She was walking out her front door and she looked really nice. No, not just nice—amazing. She had done something to her hair. It was fluffed up and shiny and she was wearing a soft pink sweater that hugged her curves and a long, slim black skirt. She looked like she was on her way out for the evening.

"You look pretty. Hot date?" he teased as he reached for one of the bags in the trunk.

She laughed nervously. "I don't know about hot, but I do have a date."

"Oh, well you look great. He's a lucky guy."

"Thanks."

"If you and the boys are available tomorrow night or Sunday, I'd love to have you all over for dinner, to thank you."

"Oh, sure. We can probably do tomorrow night. I don't think the boys have anything going on."

"I picked up some steaks and burgers as a back-up, in case they don't like steak."

"Dylan loves burgers. You didn't have to go to the trouble, though."

"It's nothing. We'll catch up tomorrow. Have fun tonight."

"Thank you." Anna got in her car and Zach watched her drive off. He grabbed the other bag and carried everything inside, wondering who her date was, and if it was the guy he'd seen her with the other day in town. He'd been on his way into the post office when he happened to look up and saw Anna and some guy coming out of The Morning Muffin and heading towards her office. He hadn't thought much of it at the time, but now thinking back, he bet that it was a lunch date. But was it serious? Or was she just getting to know him? He was surprised by the wave of jealousy that swept over him. Where did that come from? It didn't make sense as he and Anna were just friends. Obviously, he was more interested than he realized, and it seemed like someone else was, too. He would have to find out from Anna how serious things were with this other guy.

———

As Anna drove to meet Brad, she found herself thinking about Zach. She may have imagined it, but she could have sworn he almost seemed disappointed when she said she had a date tonight. If she hadn't had plans, they could have all had dinner at Zach's. They could still do it tomorrow night, so why was she feeling sad that she wasn't going to see him tonight? She had been looking forward to going out with Brad, and she knew she would have a good time with him.

He had a fun date planned for them, too. She was meeting him at Beauville's only bowling alley and they were going to play a few strings and then have dinner at Delancey's. Brad was inside the bowling alley when she arrived and was at the counter getting his rental shoes.

"Hi!" he called out when he saw her walk in. "What size shoes do you need?"

She told him and then they headed to their lane, put on their shoes and started playing. He'd suggested bowling because it was one of the things they'd both said at lunch that they liked to do, but neither had played in ages.

"So, remember when I told you I was sometimes pretty good at this?" Anna said after she threw her ball. "Obviously, I was wrong!" She watched as her ball veered sharply to the left and only managed to knock down one pin before landing in the gutter.

"You just need to warm up. It's always like that for me when I haven't played for a while."

Brad was right. She did improve a little as they went along, and although she lost badly, it was still fun.

THEY WENT TO DELANCEY'S AFTER THEY'D HAD ENOUGH bowling and were having a lovely evening until they were just about done with dessert and then Brad turned white as a ghost when a pretty woman with red hair walked by. She was with a tall, handsome man, and as she came near their table, Anna could see Brad tense up and the woman looked uncomfortable, too.

"Hello, Sophie," Brad said when they paused by their table.

"Hi Brad. You remember Rick?"

"I do. How are you?" Rick nodded hello, and then Brad turned to Anna. "Sophie, Rick, this is Anna."

"Nice to meet you," they both said at once.

"Good seeing you," Rick said and pulled Sophie along.

The energy around them was very different now. Brad looked sick to his stomach.

"Are you okay?" she asked gently, guessing that Sophie was someone who had been important to him.

"Yeah. I'm sorry. That's my ex-girlfriend. We were pretty serious for a few years. It was a hard break-up. I thought I was totally over her, and I think I am, but it just threw me seeing her with him."

"Do you know him?"

"She works with him. I'd met him at the company Christmas party." He glanced at his watch as the waiter brought the bill. He threw some money down, and then said, "Are you about ready to go?"

WHEN ANNA GOT HOME SHE CHECKED ON THE BOYS, THEN got changed and climbed into bed. She had thought there was potential with Brad, but now she wasn't so sure. He was a great guy and she enjoyed his company, but she didn't think he seemed like he was over his ex. She would go out with him again if he asked, but might want to take things even more slowly to make sure he was really ready to start dating again.

She also couldn't stop thinking about Zach and wondering how his night was, and she was looking forward to having dinner at his place with him and the boys.

The following day, there was a knock on the front door around noon, and it was Zach.

"Hi," Anna said when she opened the door.

"We should probably exchange phone numbers," Zach said. "Then we could just call instead of knocking on each other's front doors.

She laughed at that. "You're right. Here's my

number." She wrote it on a slip of paper and handed it to him and he did the same.

"Okay, so since I'm here, what I would have called to tell you is that dinner will be ready at six, so come on over.""Great, we will see you then. What can I bring?" "Nothing, just bring yourselves."

"No, I have to bring something. I'll bring a bottle of wine. Sound good?"

"If you must." Zach grinned and then turned to leave. "See you later."

Anna shut the door behind him and smiled to herself. She was looking forward to this dinner more than any other date she'd had, and this wasn't even a date.

LATER THAT AFTERNOON, ANNA WENT OVER TO ISABELLA'S house to help her pick out colors for the nursery she was decorating. Her sister, Jen, was there too and they had about a dozen paint swatches spread out over the kitchen island. They were all shades of green and yellow.

"No pinks or blues?" Anna commented as she settled into the one of the island's stools.

"No, I think I want to go gender neutral. Then I won't have to redecorate for the next baby."

"What does Travis like?" Jen asked.

"He doesn't care. Said whatever I want to do is fine."

"How's your book coming along?" Anna asked Jen. Jen was a best-selling romance novelist and often traveled to research the locations in her books.

"Good, but I'm almost at the point where I need to travel again. Heading to Ireland in a few weeks and I'll be there probably for about six weeks or so. I'll be back before the baby comes, though. I wouldn't miss that." Isabella's baby would be the first in the family, so they were all looking forward to it.

"So, tell us about your date last night," Isabella said, once they'd all agreed on a pale green shade for the nursery.

"It was great, until his ex-girlfriend walked by." She told them all about the evening, and then Jen said, "That's too bad. It sounded like it was going so well. Maybe it just took him by surprise?"

"Oh, it definitely did. He seemed devastated. I don't think he's over her. I'll go out with him again if I hear from him, but I'm really not sure he's ready to get serious with someone new."

"You never know." Isabella looked thoughtful. "It might be hard for him now, but once he realizes it is over, he might fall pretty hard for someone else. I've seen that happen quite a bit, actually, when people who have dated for a long time break up. Then within a year, one or even both of them are both engaged to other people."

"That's true, you never know. That's why I am going to try to be open-minded about it."

"What about Zach? Have you seen him around at all?"

"Actually, yes. I'm going to his place for dinner tonight."

"You have a date with him?" Isabella looked surprised and excited.

Anna immediately set her straight. "No, not a date. He invited all of us, me and the boys, to dinner, to thank us for having him over during the storm."

"Oh, okay. So it's still just friendly neighbors?"

"Right, just friends. And neighbors." She didn't mention to them that some of the thoughts she'd been having recently weren't very neighborly and that her senses were telling her that he might be slightly interested as well. He was hard to read, though, so it was difficult to tell what he was thinking.

"Oh. Well, let us know if anything more interesting develops," Jen said.

"Absolutely."

AT SIX O'CLOCK SHARP, ANNA AND THE BOYS KNOCKED ON Zach's door. He opened it and took the bottle of Cabernet that Anna held out to him.

"The man at the local wine store said that should be good with steak. I've never had it before."

"Come on in. I'll open it and let it breathe a bit." Zach led them into the kitchen, where he poured a couple of Cokes for the boys and showed them how to turn on the TV in the family room.

"You've settled in well. Looks like you've been here for ages," Anna said as she looked around the room.

"Most of this stuff was already here. I rented it

furnished, but the few things that I do have are all unpacked finally. It took me a full week."

"Moving isn't fun. I can't imagine how long it would take me now if I had to move. We've accumulated so much stuff over the years." She walked to the back of the kitchen, where it opened onto the deck. "I've always admired the windows on this place. They're so big and the views are incredible." The windows were floor-to-ceiling and let in tons of light.

"I agree. I'm hoping to do something similar with the remodel on my uncle's place."

"That's a great idea. How is it coming along so far?"

"Good, but it's early stages, still. Just this week, they ripped off the roof and are getting ready to build out the second floor." That sounded like a major remodel to Anna.

"How much bigger will it be?" she asked.

"Adding the second floor and expanding the first some will more than double the square footage. It will have four large bedrooms when I finish. Right now, it just has two small ones."

"What are you going to do with all that space?" Anna wondered out loud.

"That's the part I haven't decided yet. I'm either going to build it out, stage and sell it. Or keep it and move there when my lease here is up."

"Are you seriously considering keeping it? And moving here permanently?"

"I'm considering it." He grinned, and added, "It depends on which day you ask me and how things are going." He walked over to the wine, then and poured two glasses for them then handed her one.

"Are you getting hungry yet?"

"A little bit. Can I help you do anything?"

"No, just relax. There's not much to do. I just need to throw the meat on the grill. The potatoes are in the oven and there's steamed broccoli and carrots."

"That sounds wonderful." Anna's stomach rumbled in appreciation.

The steaks were delicious, and after they all ate, Zach brought out a deck of cards and taught them all how to play Pitch. Anna had played years ago and it came right back to her. The boys were a little frustrated at first, but once they got the hang of it, they really liked it, especially when Dylan won the first game. They played at the kitchen table and Zach had a fire going in the wood stove nearby.

"I'm well-stocked now, so there's no danger of being cold when the next storm hits," he said as he added another log to the stove.

They played for several hours, until Dylan started to yawn and Anna realized how late it was, already past ten o'clock.

"We should get going. I need to get these guys to bed. Thank you for having us over. This was really fun."

Zach walked them to the door. "What are you all doing tomorrow?" he asked.

Anna thought about it for a moment. "We're going to church in the morning and then nothing planned after that. The boys probably have some homework they need to do at some point, and I'll be doing laundry and other fun stuff like that. Typical Sunday."

"Do you want to take a ride with me out to my uncle's place? The boys can come, too. It looks like it's going to be a clear day and I'd love to show it to you."

"Sure, we'd love to." Anna then impulsively said, "Do you go to church, Zach? Why don't you come with us in the morning and then we can go see your place after that?"

Zach hesitated. "I haven't been to church in a long time. Maybe it's time I made a visit."

CHAPTER 8

Z ach hadn't been to church in a very long time. He'd gone a few times after the accident, trying to make sense of it all and trying to find answers wherever he could. He didn't find them in church, though, and stopped going. He rode with Anna and the boys and was surprised by how he felt when they walked into the church. It was just a sense of immediate comfort and rightness. He couldn't have explained it if he tried, other than to simply just say he felt warmth sink into him as he settled in a pew with Anna and the boys.

After the service, they stopped for lunch at a local sub shop and then drove out to see Zach's project. He directed Anna to turn down the long driveway and as they drew near the house, the boys started paying attention.

"Is this all yours? Your yard is huge!" Her older son, Tom, sounded impressed.

"It's about a hundred acres," Zach said as parked the car. They all got out, and the boys immediately started exploring. Zach led her over to the house, which was in a state of disarray with the roof gone.

"Watch your step. There's stuff all over the place," Zach said as he led her into the house and showed her around. He explained his vision and he could tell from her eyes that she was proud of him, which both confused him and made him ridiculously happy. Why would she be proud of him? He must have misread or imagined what he'd seen.

"Did you have fun on your date the other night?" he asked, wondering if she was dating anyone seriously.

"I did have fun. Well, for most of the date, anyway. It was just the second time we'd gone out and it was going really well, until we ran into his ex-girlfriend." She filled him in and then added, "I'm not sure if he's completely over her. It didn't seem that way."

"What about you? Is there anyone back home waiting for you?"

That gave him pause for a moment, thinking about his lunch with Bethanne.

"No. There was, but it ended when I moved here. It never really felt like we were with the right person."

"I understand." Zach could tell she was thinking of someone, probably her ex-husband who wasn't a perfect fit, either.

"So, what are you thinking you will do with all this land?" Anna asked, and Zach guessed she was trying to change the subject to something less personal.

"A few different options. I could subdivide and sell off smaller lots, develop them myself, or add on to them and build a ranch of my own. Or maybe take over an existing one. I'm still thinking about all of them."

"Sounds like some big decisions are coming." Anna smiled as she looked around the property. "It's a beautiful spot. Whatever you decide to do, I'm sure it will be a success."

"I hope you're right."

ANNA FELT A CHILL ACROSS HER SPINE AS ZACH SHOWED her around his property. Everything he talked about, his plans for the property, possibly doing some real estate development, even owning a ranch, were all dreams they'd discussed over and over again. She was proud of him that he was trying to make those dreams come true, and that he'd seen his uncle's land as a sign to come home, even if he didn't fully understand why. She just wished he'd remember. She wanted so badly to tell him how much she'd loved him then and how much he had loved her, too. She felt her eyes water and turned away for a moment to collect herself. Zach was right there, though, almost as if he'd sensed it.

"Is everything okay?" he asked when he saw her watery eyes.

She smiled and nodded. "Totally fine. A cold blast of air just hit my eyes."

Zach watched her intently for a moment, and then let it go.

"Are you guys ready to head back, then? That temperature is dropping fast."

They got home about three and said their goodbyes to Zach. Anna got busy around the house, doing laundry and getting a pot of chili going for dinner while the boys started on their homework. They ate at five, and as Anna was cleaning up and packing the chili into plastic containers to go into the refrigerator, she wondered what Zach was doing for dinner. She had so much leftover chili. She decided to run a container over to him and realized that she was starting to have it bad. She just wanted to see him. It wasn't enough that they'd spent most of the day together.

She put the rest of the chili away and left one container out that she put into a bag, and then told the boys she'd be right back.

She started to get nervous as she walked up to his door. What if he didn't like chili? Or had already eaten? Or was just sick of seeing her?

He answered the door and smiled when he saw her and she relaxed.

"I didn't know if you'd eaten yet or not, but I made chili this afternoon and we had tons of leftovers, so I brought you some." She handed him the bag with the container.

"Can you come in for a minute? I just poured a glass of wine and was thinking about what to have for dinner and realized nothing I have is appealing. Until now." His eyes met hers and she felt a charge of something between them.

"I can only stay for a few minutes. The chili is still hot if you want to eat it now."

"Sure, but only if you have a glass of wine with me to keep me company while I eat."

"Twist my arm," she agreed.

He poured a glass of red wine for her, and she joined him in the kitchen and took the seat closest to the wood stove.

"You're not too hot there?" Zach asked as he dipped his spoon in the chili.

"No, it feels great. I love the heat."

"This is excellent. Thank you."

They chatted comfortably while he ate, and then he put the container with the rest of the chili in his refrigerator.

"I'll think of you when I have that for lunch tomorrow."

"I should probably head back over there. The boys might be looking for me."

"It would be more fun if you stayed. I've really enjoyed hanging out with you. But, I understand. It is a school night."

Anna felt the same. She really wanted to stay. She just liked being with Zach.

"I'd love to stay longer, but I did tell them I'd be right back." She stood to walk to the door.

Zach stood too, and gave her a hug goodbye. They both held on a little longer than necessary, and when Anna pulled back, their eyes met and she could tell that they both felt the connection. Zach leaned in and let his lips lightly brush against hers and she melted into him. He pulled her in tightly then, and really kissed her deeply. He finally lifted his head and stepped back with a dazed look on his face.

"Well, that was unexpected, but kind of amazing."

"Kind of?" she teased. She was in a bit of a daze herself. It had been over twenty years since she'd last kissed Zach, and all the familiar feelings had come rushing back. And if anything, were stronger, and more mature. It was a lot to process.

"Definitely amazing," he said.

"Goodnight, Zach."

"I'll talk to you soon."

Zach closed the door and reached for his wine glass. He still had half a glass and he needed it. What the hell had just happened? He went into the family room, turned on the TV and then stared at it, not really seeing it but just hearing the white noise of the news anchors as they spoke. He'd never experienced anything like that kiss before. He knew he was attracted to Anna, but what they'd just shared was off the charts. But there was something else going on, too. It wasn't just physical attraction —it was as if he really knew her, had always known her. It didn't make sense at all, and truth be told, it scared him a little.

CHAPTER 9

"We kissed. He kissed me. It wasn't planned. It was just one of those impulsive things. I brought him chili." Anna knew that she was rambling. She and Isabella were in Anna's office and they only had a minute to catch up, so Anna let it all out in a rush.

"That must have been some really good chili," Isabella teased.

"Very funny. It was just unexpected, I think, for both of us. Zach especially. He really looked odd when I left."

"Maybe kissing you again brought back memories?" Isabella said.

"I wondered the same thing. I've been waiting to see if being back here would shake any of those memories loose. I thought as he saw people he knew from back then it might help too, but I think so far, I am the only one he's really run into."

Isabella thought about that for a moment.

"Do any of his close friends from high school still live here?"

"No, just me. His best friends Teddy and Jim both live out of state now."

"Well, he was in the same year as Christian and Travis, right?"

"He was, but he wasn't tight with them then."

"But still, it's something. Ah-ha! I've got it." Isabella slammed her hand down on Anna's desk, making her jump.

"What is it?"

"The teachers' appreciation event is in two weeks at the high school. It's a Sunday afternoon pizza and cake party and all the retired teachers who are still in the area usually drop in. What about that?"

"Now, that is a good idea." Anna loved the sound of it. Zach had a few teachers who he really liked and who had encouraged him in school. Seeing some of them again could be the kind of catalyst that would help loosen up some of those old memories.

"So, what do you think of it? Might be kind of fun for you to go back to school and see where you spent so many years." Zach had stopped by after work to return the chili container and Anna told him about the teacher event.

"It's on a Sunday? I should be able to do that. Only if you go with me, though. You'll have to introduce me to everyone." He looked sheepish as he said it, and she chuckled.

"I can do that."

Zach leaned against the kitchen counter while Anna continued to load her dishwasher. She and the boys had just finished eating dinner and now she was cleaning up.

"You know, I think I might be starting to remember things, a little," Zach said.

Anna stopped what she was doing to turn and face him.

"What have you remembered?"

"It's just little things, nothing of any real importance. Just flashes of memory. Like I went to the library here the other day to make some copies because my printer was down and when I walked in the door, I knew exactly where the copy machines were. I even recognized one of the ladies behind the front desk. Or maybe she recognized me first, but she did look sort of familiar."

"That's great. Have you remembered anything else?"

"No, but I keep having this sense that there is something really big that is just outside my grasp. It's frustrating, because I have no idea what it is." Anna felt a chill run up her spine.

"Maybe if you just don't try so hard, it'll come easier. Just relax and see what comes to you."

"I suppose. I just feel like I'm so close to some kind of a breakthrough at times, and then the feeling slips away."

"It will come in time. You have to believe that. Maybe the teacher event will help."

"Maybe," he agreed. "So, let's do something this

weekend. Go into Bozeman for the night. we can go see a show or something. I'm feeling stir-crazy. Do you ever feel that way?"

"I'm too busy to feel stir-crazy," she laughed. "I have kids."

"Okay, I'll give you that. But still, it would be fun to get out don't you think?"

"It does sound fun."

Zach looked forward to Friday night all week. He and Anna had made plans to head into Bozeman right after work, grab a bite to eat and then see a comedy show after.

He knocked on Anna's door just before six, and then they headed out. She looked great, with her hair in a loose braid and a pretty, cream-colored sweater, snug jeans and cowboy boots.

Anna suggested a small Italian restaurant that looked like a dive from the outside but was tiny and charming inside, and the smells were intoxicating. The food tasted even better. They shared an appetizer tray of assorted meats, cheeses and stuffed mushrooms, and then a pasta platter with three types of homemade pastas, cheese tortellini, rigatoni and gnocchi—then their entree platter of chicken piccata and veal parmesan. Everything was served family style and they had as much as they wanted. By the time they walked out, they were absolutely stuffed and welcomed the walk to the comedy show, which was several blocks away.

Once they were seated inside, Anna was surprised to see a table of familiar faces right next to them. It was a group of teachers, some of them the ones that she was hoping to see the following week at the school event.

She said hello to all of them and then introduced Zach.

"Zach recently moved back to Beauville. Some of you may remember him from when you were teaching."

"You were on the debate team, weren't you?" asked Mr. Roberts.

"I was, yes." Zach answered.

"I saw you win at regionals against Bozeman. You did a great job that year for us."

"I always enjoyed the debate team," Zach said.

"You doing something out at your uncle's place? Or did it get sold?" Ed Smith, the oldest of the teachers there, was nearly ninety and often said he was too old to not say what was on his mind.

"I'm doing a little remodeling out there."

"Looks like more than a little, young man. That's quite a project. You going to sell or keep that for yourself?"

"I'm still trying to figure that out. I'm not sure."

"Hmmm," was all Mr. Smith had to add to that.

The lights dimmed then, indicating it was time to sit down and for the show to start. Anna and Zach sat at their table and both ordered Cokes when the waitress came by. They'd each had two glasses of wine at the restaurant, so neither one wanted another drink, especially if they were going to be driving the half-hour back to Beauville.

The comedy show was excellent. Some of the comedians were funnier than others and Anna couldn't remember the last time she'd laughed so hard. Zach drove home and he'd been quiet most of the way. When they pulled in the driveway he turned to her.

"Come inside for a while. I have dessert for us. Chocolate ice cream, and something made me buy chocolate sprinkles and whipped cream, too. An odd combination, I know, but we can pretend it's something special."

He's starting to remember, Anna realized. When she was in high school, that was her favorite way to eat ice cream. It was always chocolate and she'd cover it with whipped cream and sprinkles.

"Okay, I'll come in. But only because you have ice cream."

Once they were inside, Zach scooped the ice cream into two small bowls and then handed her a spoon.

"What about the whipped cream and sprinkles?" she asked.

"Do you really want them?" He sounded surprised.

"Of course I do. That's what you said dessert was."

He handed her the can of whipped cream and she made a perfect mound on top of her ice cream and then dusted it with sprinkles.

"Want me to do yours?" she asked.

He chuckled. "I'm good."

They took their ice cream into the family room and sat next to each other on the sofa. When they finished, Anna moved to get up and bring their bowls into the kitchen but Zach put his hand on her leg.

"Relax, we can bring the bowls out later. Just set them on the end table for now. And come here." He pulled her close to him. "I had a great time tonight." He leaned in and kissed her—gently at first, and she could taste chocolate ice cream. Soon she forgot about ice cream, though, and got lost in the heat of kissing Zach. The kiss went on for quite a while until it either needed to turn into something else, or end. When they came up for air, Anna sensed it was best for her to go, before things went somewhere that she didn't think either of them was emotionally ready to handle.

"Do you have plans tomorrow?" he asked.

Anna thought for a moment, then remembered the boys were away with their dad for the weekend so she was completely free.

"What did you have in mind?"

"Want to take a road trip to Billings? I have this charity gala thing I was going to blow off, but if you're up for it, it might be kind of fun. We can make a night of it and stay at my house in town and then drive back tomorrow."

"I'm in. What time do we leave?"

CHAPTER 10

They set out around three the next afternoon. The drive to Billings would take a little over two hours, and Zach had suggested they go to his house first and relax. Take their time getting ready and then take a cab over to The Carlyle where the event was being held. Anna was excited. She almost never went to things like this and had stopped by Isabella's earlier that morning to borrow a dress. Isabella had a closet full of dresses for her to choose from. It was almost like being in a store. The winning dress was a basic, black cocktail dress, slimming and sleek in a satiny fabric and with the tiniest spaghetti straps. It was flattering on and made her look a good five pounds thinner, which was a nice bonus.

They made the most of a long, boring car ride by singing along to the radio at the top of their lungs. Zach seemed surprised to discover that they shared a lot of the same musical favorites and seemed to know all the words to the same songs. Anna just smiled to herself. He was getting so close to figuring it all out.

When they arrived in Billings, Zach drove to a condo downtown. It was almost an exact replica to the one she'd shown him in Beauville, except it was a little less vanilla. His unit was spacious and had top of the line finishings—granite countertops, all stainless steel appliances, polished hard wood floors. It was immaculate and there was no clutter anywhere. It almost looked like it hadn't been lived in, but then Anna noticed the colorful artwork that hung on the walls in the small room he used as a home office. Some of it looked familiar and she walked over to get a closer look.

She recognized one of the pieces as soon as she got closer to it. Zach had painted it during his senior year. He'd always loved art classes and could spend hours working on a painting and trying to get just the right shade of green. He often lost all track of time when he was painting. The other paintings along the wall looked similar in style, but she hadn't seen them before. She wondered if he'd continued to paint over the years or if these were all from before the accident.

"These are lovely."

"Thanks. I actually did those many years ago. I haven't painted in years or felt any desire to, but it seems at one time, I really enjoyed it."

"You don't remember painting these?" Anna's heart broke for him. It was something he had loved so very much. It pained her to think he had lost that.

"I have a feeling about them. When I look at them, I

feel joy and I think that must be what I felt when I did them. But, the memories themselves haven't come back. I haven't tried to paint either, though. I haven't really felt the strong urge to do it. But maybe I will try sometime."

"I'll do it with you, if you want some company. I used to like to paint, too. I'm nowhere near as talented, though. My efforts look more like paint-by-numbers. I always had fun doing it, though." She smiled, remembering how she would often spend an afternoon at Zach's —they'd be down in the basement, paints everywhere, and they'd stay there for hours. Anna would play with her painting and sneak glances at Zach's every now and then. He was in his own world—the zone, as he used to call it, when everything else just fell away and he was in a dream state of sorts. She could always tell when he 'went away' to that place and she was content to just be there with him. She hoped that he'd find that magic again. Painting would be a great hobby for him to pick up and to relax with.

"So, what is the charity this gala is raising money for?"

"Alzheimer's. My former partner started it, actually, in honor of his grandfather who passed away from Alzheimer's the year we opened our office here. That was a tough year for him. Doing this, doing something to try and help, is his way of remembering his grandfather and giving back."

"Do they raise a lot of money?"

Zach chuckled. "Tons. Rob has a bunch of friends in New York who are in the investment business. A few started a hedge fund that did really well and they have more money than they'll ever need. They don't mind sharing it. Every year, they all fly out for this and make a long weekend out of it.

"That sounds like fun."

"It usually is a good time. We should probably start getting ready."

———

AN HOUR LATER, AFTER GRABBING A CAB, THEY PULLED UP in front of The Carlyle. Anna didn't think that she'd ever been to a more luxurious hotel. They went first to the hotel bar, where Zach's former partner and his friends were gathering before heading in to the gala. Zach introduced her around. They all seemed very nice, but their names went right in one ear and out the other. Zach asked her what she wanted to drink and while she was waiting, she decided to get comfortable. There were plush, brown leather chairs at the polished oak bar and when Anna sat down in one of them, she sank into the soft leather. It was wonderful. When the bartender returned with their drinks, he also had a small, silver jar of hot, salted nuts for them to nibble on.

"I could get used to this," Anna said to Zach and he grinned. "You haven't seen anything yet."

He led the way into the main ballroom where the event was being held and for the next few hours, they were dazzled by an array of passed hot appetizers, chilled raw bar and then, once they were seated for dinner, it seemed like the courses kept coming. The food was outstanding. Once dinner was over and dessert had been served and cleared, the band started playing and people made their way onto the dance floor.

Anna took a bathroom break and while she was in a stall in the ladies' room, she overheard two women talking.

"I'm surprised that Bethanne's not here," one of them said.

"Yes, especially since it's her fiance's partner's gala. Although Zach seems to have someone else with him. Do you know her?"

"No, I've never seen her before. Maybe it's just a friend."

"Friends who come to galas like this? I doubt it, although Bethanne is still flashing that diamond ring and telling everyone she's hoping to have the wedding here."

"Strange."

Anna waited until the two women left before coming out of the restroom. She needed to talk to Zach.

He must have seen by the look on her face that something was wrong as she walked toward the table.

"What is it?" he said as soon as she sat down.

"I can't talk about it here. Can we go now?"

"Sure, I was going to suggest it, anyway. It's getting late."

Zach was able to get a cab quickly, and less than fifteen minutes later they were walking into his condo. He immediately pulled her into his arms. "What is it? What's wrong?" Anna stiffened and took a step back.

"Who is Bethanne?"

Anna noticed his jaw clench, but he spoke calmly as he said, "Bethanne is my ex-girlfriend."

"Were you engaged?"

"Yes. But I broke it off."

"Then why is she still telling people that you're engaged? And wearing your ring? What's really going on?"

Zach sighed and then told her the whole story of Bethanne.

"So, I told her she could keep the ring. She said she deserved it and I guess she did. I mean, I did ask her to marry me. I never should have done that. I regretted it almost immediately."

Anna sat down and just looked at Zach. All her anger was gone, just like that.

"It just threw me. I knew it didn't make sense. You've never lied to me before." That might not have made a lot of sense to him, but it did to her. Zach never had lied to her as long as she'd known him. She was more upset at the fact that he'd been engaged to someone else. She didn't like feeling jealous, especially when it didn't seem to be warranted.

"Come here for a minute. I have something to tell you." Zach reached out, took her hand and led her into his office where there was a small couch. He turned on the light and they both sat.

"This is my favorite room, and I've been thinking about what I was going to say all week. There's something

I've been dying to tell you, but it had to be the right time."

"What is it?" He looked so serious that she started to feel nervous. But then he smiled and his eyes lit up. Her heart melted again as she looked into his eyes.

"I remember."

She felt the hair on the back of her neck stand up.

"What do you remember?" she whispered.

"I remember you and us. I remember us, and I am so sorry for what I must have put you through."

Tears started to fall down her cheeks as he continued to talk.

"The night we came back from Bozeman and saw those old teachers at the show and then had ice cream—it was just things starting to come together. I knew about the ice cream, but I didn't know about you then, not yet. I dreamed that night. Vivid dreams—a lot of them didn't make any sense, but before I woke up everything came into focus and it was you. Memories of us in high school, talking about our dreams and our future. It just all came rushing back."

He reached into his pocket then and pulled out a small, pale blue box. He got down on one knee and he opened it—Anna almost passed out when she saw the diamond.

"I know I don't deserve you, but I'm asking anyway. Anna, will you marry me? So we can make the dreams those two high school kids had come true? It doesn't have to be right away, just sometime in the future?"

As soon as Anna was able to stop crying and compose herself, she finally managed to say, "Of course I will."

He slid the diamond ring on her finger and she couldn't stop staring at it. It was beautiful, but it was also completely surreal.

"I'm glad you got me my own ring," she finally managed to say.

Zach laughed at that. "You deserve that, and so much more! I love you. I just had no idea how much and for how long."

"I feel like I have always loved you. It's always been you." The tears started to flow again as the realization of what was happening sunk in.

"I think I need to kiss those tears away."

"They're tears of happiness," she assured him. "But you can kiss me anyway."

"Here's to spending the rest of our lives together, starting now."

And then he kissed her…

EPILOGUE

THREE MONTHS LATER.....

"I am so ready for this baby to come out!" Isabella said. They were all at Anna's house for a Jack and Jill shower. Isabella's due date was two months away and she was huge and feeling it. They'd had lunch, cake and now had moved on to opening presents. Jen was sitting by Isabella's feet with a trash bag on one side of her and a notebook on the other, so she could dispose of the pretty wrapping paper and then jot down who had given what gifts. They'd gotten through all the gifts except for one.

"We couldn't really wrap ours, so we're just going to give it to you," Anna said as she nodded at her husband. She and Zach had gone to see the justice of the peace the week after they'd returned from Billings and made it official. Neither one of them had wanted to wait. Zach had sublet his rental and moved in with Anna the same week.

Eventually, once the extensive renovations were done on his Uncle's property, they'd all be moving there as a family. Zach had decided to keep the land and follow his dream by starting a small ranch while continuing to run his consulting business remotely.

He walked to the guest room and returned a moment later with what looked like a large painting. When he turned it around, the room grew silent and Isabella's eyes grew misty, though she was more emotional than usual these days because of the hormones.

"Anna and I made this for the baby's room."

"I can't really take any credit for that. I just kept telling him he was doing a great job," Anna laughed.

"She did more than that. She was with me most of the time I painted this, working on her own painting."

"His won." Anna said, and everyone laughed.

"Seriously, though, she is my inspiration and the reason I was able to start painting again." Anna's heart swelled. Zach was painting again and she loved spending a Sunday afternoon just being with him and watching him work.

"It's beautiful. Thank you both," Isabella said.

Zach came and sat back down next to Anna and squeezed her hand.

"I meant that, you know. Just having you beside me is all I'll ever need. I love you."

"I'm so happy you came back to me."

~The End~

Please visit my website, www.pamelakelley.com to see all my books—including my newest, Nantucket Weddings and The Restaurant. You can also sign up for email notifications there and see news on my blog. Thanks so much! =)

ABOUT THE AUTHOR

Pamela M. Kelley is a USA Today and Wall Street Journal bestselling author. Readers often describe her books as feel-good reads with people you'd want as friends.

She lives in a historic seaside town near Cape Cod and just south of Boston. She has always been an avid reader of women's fiction, romance, mysteries, thrillers and cook books. There's also a good chance you might get hungry when you read her books as she is a foodie, and occasionally shares a recipe or two.

Made in the USA
Monee, IL
29 May 2021

69734920R00062